THE LITTLE BLACK HEN

Story by Lene Hille-Brandts
Pictures by Sigrid Heuck
Adapted by Marion Koenig

 CHILDRENS PRESS, CHICAGO

LENE HILLE-BRANDTS wrote a number of books before her death in 1958. Although few of these were published during her lifetime, ten of her books are now in print.

SIGRID HEUCK first studied fashion designing, then went to the Munich Academy of Arts for four years. She now works as a freelance artist and has six books to her credit—the first of which won a silver medal at the Triennale in Milan in 1960.

Library of Congress Catalog Card Number: 68-31313

Original title: Die Henne Gudula
Copyright © by Annette Betz, München, 1965
English text Copyright © by W. & R. Chambers, Edinburgh, 1967

American edition published 1968 by
Regensteiner Publishing Enterprises, Inc.
All Rights Reserved   Printed in U.S.A.
Published simultaneously in Canada

THE LITTLE BLACK HEN

Once upon a time there was a little black hen. She lived in a farmyard, but she was not happy there.

"It is flurry, scurry, all day long. There is never any time for fun in this farmyard. The animals in the woods have time for fun. Today they are giving a party. I want to go too," she said to herself.

She preened her feathers so that she would look her best for the party. Then, when no one was looking, she ran out of the farmyard and down to the woods.

All the animals were there. She saw the geese, the foxes, the pigs, the rabbits, the owls, and many others.

The woodpecker took one look at the little black hen's glossy feathers and asked her for the first dance.

After that, the little black hen danced with all the other animals. She had a wonderful time at the party and did not get home until dawn.

The rooster, who was guarding the farmyard, was very angry with the little black hen. He stood outside the coop with his tail spread.

"This will not do," he shouted. "Hens who stay out all night are not allowed here. Be off at once."

The little black hen was frightened and ran back to the woods. She felt very sorry for herself.

The woodpeckers saw her and felt very sorry for her too. "Why don't you move in with us, little black hen?" they said. "There is plenty of room and we would enjoy your company."

So the little black hen moved in with the woodpeckers. She was happy in her new home.

At first the woodland animals thought it odd to see a farmyard hen living in a tree. But when they were used to the idea, they soon made friends with the little black hen. Some of them even went into the fields with her to look for food.

But a field is no place for a little farmyard hen. One day a farmer who was plowing caught sight of her.

"You'll do for my supper," he said. Reaching out, he caught her around the neck with one hand.

Then the farmer popped a basket over her. It was dark under the basket and the little black hen was frightened.

Luckily, a mouse saw what happened. Feeling sorry for the little black hen, the mouse came to her rescue.

First the mouse burrowed under the basket. Then she helped the little black hen to squeeze out through the tunnel she had made.

Off ran the mouse and the little black hen before the farmer could catch them.

All summer and fall the little black hen lived in the tree with the woodpeckers. She felt very safe there, hidden behind the leaves. But when winter came, and all the leaves were gone from the trees, the branches were cold and bare.

One day two huntsmen came past. They saw the little black hen sitting in the tree. At first they thought she was a crow. One of them raised his gun and took aim.

"Oh dear," cackled the little black hen. She flapped her wings, but she was too heavy to fly.

"My goodness! It's a *hen*," said the huntsmen. They lifted the little black hen out of the tree and tied a string to her leg. Then they led her away.

The huntsmen took the little black hen to their cottage. There they tied her to a doghouse.

"You shall be our watchdog," they said. "You must give the alarm if you see anyone coming."

It was warmer in the doghouse than it had been out in the woods, but the little black hen felt lonely.

One night she saw two strangers creeping up to the cottage. For a moment she was quite glad to see them. But when one of them raised a hammer to break a window, she remembered what the two huntsmen had told her to do. Cackling loudly, she rushed out and pecked at their legs.

The strangers turned pale. They had never seen a pecking, fluttering, cackling watchdog before. They dropped their ladder and hammer and ran away as fast as they could.

The huntsmen were pleased. They gave the little black hen a big feast of corn. They also told her she could visit her friends in the woods whenever she liked.

From that day on, the little black hen lived happily in her home with the huntsmen.